W9-ALX-415

Kamehameha

The Boy Who Became A Warrior King

Written by Ellie Crowe

Illustrated by Don Robinson

To Will, with love and thanks for your research and suggestions.

Published and distributed by

ISLAND HERITAGE
PUBLISHING

94-411 KŌʻAKI STREET, WAIPAHU, HAWAIʻI 96797
ORDERS: (800) 468-2800 • INFORMATION: (808) 564-8800
FAX: (808) 564-8877 • www.islandheritage.com

ISBN 0-89610-567-9
First Edition, First Printing - 2003

ACKNOWLEDGMENTS:

Thank you Professor Rubellite Kawena Johnson for your help with my story on the childhood of the beloved Hawaiian monarch, Kamehameha the Great.

THE FARAWAY VALLEY

Climbing swiftly, the young boy pulled himself up to the top of the huge breadfruit tree, where the branches swayed and dipped wildly in the wind. Sitting there among the leaves and swinging balls of fruit, he could see the whole valley, so green and so lonely. He wished he had a friend, a boy who would dive into the surf and swim with him—a boy who liked to climb trees.

Looking up at the high, dark cliffs, he shivered. Why did he always feel that there was danger around him? Why was he never allowed to leave the valley? Why did the warrior Nae'ole guard him so carefully? What was Nae'ole so afraid of?

One morning he joined Nae'ole as he sat sharpening a spear at the water's edge. "I wish I could leave the valley, Nae'ole," he said. "I wish I could visit my mother and father. I've never seen them. Not even once. Nae'ole, please tell me, why do I always have to stay hidden?"

Nae'ole sighed. "I know that you would like to leave our valley, Pai'ea, but you must not. Your uncle, King Alapa'i, means to kill you."

"Kill me! But why would my uncle want to kill me?"

"I will tell you," Nae'ole said. "You are five now. I think you are old enough to understand. You are a special child, my chief. On the night that you were born there was a strange sign. A large star appeared—a huge shining star with a long tail of fiery light. Everyone knew then."

"Knew what?"

"That you would be a very important person. A *kahuna,* a priest, warned King Alapa'i that you, a newborn baby, would one day be a powerful warrior, a conqueror who would be king of all the islands. A killer of kings."

The young boy's heart beat fast as he listened to this strange story.

"Alapa'i wanted to get rid of you then, Pai'ea. He called his warriors and ordered them to find you. Your mother was sick with fear. As soon as you were born, she wrapped you in soft *kapa* cloth and gave you to me. I ran all that dark stormy night, across fields and through the forests, down into this valley. You were just a tiny, tiny baby."

"Did the warriors look for me?"

"They hunted for you for weeks. One frightening night I heard them coming near. I hid you, hoping you would not cry. It was a terrible night, but you were so good. You didn't make a sound, and they passed by."

"Did the *kahuna* really say that I would be a powerful warrior, Nae'ole? Did he really say that I would be the warrior king of all the islands?"

Nae'ole laughed. "Yes he did. But you are still only a boy. You need to become much stronger to become a warrior king. Come, I'll race you to the waterfall."

"Can we practice *lua* instead?" Pai'ea asked, jumping high and kicking hard. The world outside the valley sounded strange and dangerous. He wanted to be very strong before he faced it.

THE COURT OF KING ALAPA'I

It was early morning and mists swirled in the valley. Pai'ea yawned as he walked outside, rubbing his arms to keep warm. His foster mother and Nae'ole sat close together, whispering and looking worried. When they saw him they became silent.

"What's happening?" Pai'ea asked.

"My chief, the time has come for you to return to the court of King Alapa'i and live with your parents," Nae'ole said.

"But you said King Alapa'i wants to kill me, Nae'ole! How can I go there?"

"Don't worry. I will be there to protect you," Nae'ole said. "Alapa'i is old and feeble now, and they say he no longer fears you."

That dark, moonless night, Nae'ole and Pai'ea climbed the high cliffs out of the valley. The wind wailed, and trees groaned and swayed.

By the time they arrived at the village, it was late afternoon. Pai'ea was tired, and Nae'ole carried him on his shoulders. They walked slowly past grass houses, coconut trees, and flowering shrubs. The many chatting people grew silent and stared with curiosity in their eyes.

As they reached a circle of large houses, a beautiful woman and a tall man came toward them, holding out their arms in welcome.

"My son!" the woman said. "It's been such a long, long time."

Pai'ea clung to Nae'ole's arm, feeling very shy. He was not used to so many strange people. This was his own mother! His own father! He didn't know what to say to them.

An old man wearing a long feathered cape came out of a large house. Pai'ea knew this must be King Alapa'i. He watched with interest as some people bowed down before the king. Others removed most of their clothing and lay facing the ground. An attendant followed behind the king, jumping forward with a bowl every time the king cleared his throat.

"The king is afraid of the magic of sorcerers," Nae'ole said. "The attendant is safeguarding the king's spit."

Pai'ea nodded solemnly. The attendant had an important job, but he was glad he didn't have to do it.

The king walked over and greeted him, looking him slowly up and down. Silent, Pai'ea bent his head respectfully. Did King Alapa'i still want to kill him?

"Come and eat now, my son," Pai'ea's mother said. "You must be hungry after your long journey here." Pai'ea stood at Nae'ole's side, not knowing what to do. The roasting pig smelled good and he was hungry, but he didn't know which house to go to. Was he old enough to eat with the men of the court?

King Alapa'i looked at him coldly and laughed. "What a shy boy. Let us call him Kamehameha, the lonely one."

Pai'ea knew then that Alapa'i still hated him.

"It's a strong name," Nae'ole whispered. "A name for a warrior king."

Nae'ole was right—Kamehameha was a strong name. Pai'ea smiled at his mother, and she smiled back.

"You will train to be a young warrior soon, Kamehameha," she said. "You will eat with the men."

After the meal, Kamehameha sat contentedly with Nae'ole, licking the juice of the baked pig off his fingers.

A group of older boys came walking down the path, stopping when they saw Nae'ole and Kamehameha. "So you are my new cousin," a tall, stout boy said. "I don't like your face." He and his friends began laughing.

"Your new cousin never laughs, Keawe'opala," a big boy mocked. "I guess he doesn't like us."

Kamehameha took a deep breath and walked forward, facing his cousin with his legs apart and his hands on his hips. Keawe'opala pushed at his chest, and he pushed back as hard as he could.

"Wait," Nae'ole said. "Why don't you challenge your cousin to a hand-wrestling match?" Kamehameha nodded; Nae'ole had trained him well in the art of *uma*.

"All right, I challenge you," he said to Keawe'opala.

"You'll lose," his cousin replied. "You are weak, like a girl." The other boys laughed loudly.

The two boys took their positions lying in the sand and placed their hands together. Muscles bulging, Keawe'opala pushed hard against Kamehameha's arm. Kamehameha pushed back as hard as he could. Suddenly, bang! Kamehameha's arm went into the sand. He'd lost.

"I challenge you again," he said.

"So you enjoy losing," Keawe'opala jeered. They clenched hands again. Sweat ran down their faces as their arms went back and forth. Kamehameha pushed and pushed, and bang! Keawe'opala's arm hit the sand. Trying to hide a triumphant grin, Kamehameha stood up to walk away—then he heard Nae'ole's warning. Keawe'opala was coming at him with a long stick. Kamehameha grabbed the stick and used the force of Keawe'opala's jump to fling him off. How lucky that he was skilled at *lua,* the best way of fighting! Keawe'opala fell, hitting the dirt with a thud.

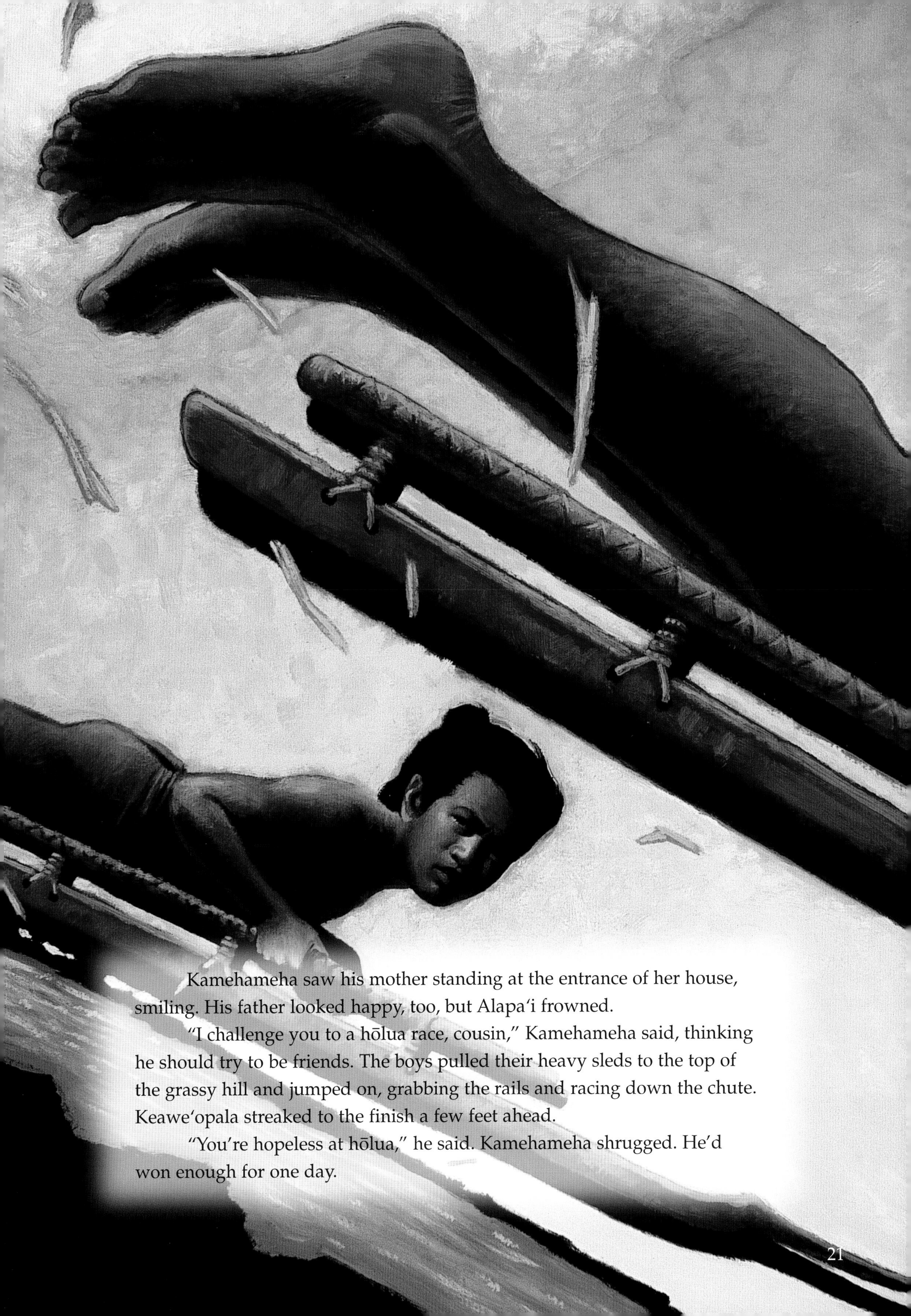

Kamehameha saw his mother standing at the entrance of her house, smiling. His father looked happy, too, but Alapa'i frowned.

"I challenge you to a hōlua race, cousin," Kamehameha said, thinking he should try to be friends. The boys pulled their heavy sleds to the top of the grassy hill and jumped on, grabbing the rails and racing down the chute. Keawe'opala streaked to the finish a few feet ahead.

"You're hopeless at hōlua," he said. Kamehameha shrugged. He'd won enough for one day.

Kamehameha started to train to be a warrior and Keawe'opala trained, too. They wrestled, surfed, swam, hand wrestled and chest pushed.

"King Alapa'i is the most powerful king on this island," Keawe'opala said one day. "He killed your grandfather. He doesn't like you. You'd better be careful you don't make him mad."

"I'm not afraid," Kamehameha said. "Maybe one day I will be powerful, too."

Keawe'opala laughed so much that he fell on the ground, clutching his stomach. Afterward, he said he had a terrible stomachache. He said it was all Kamehameha's fault.

For the next five years, Kamehameha spent most of his time with Nae'ole. He kept out of King Alapa'i's way. His parents were busy, and he didn't see them often. His life was happy, but when he was eleven years old, a terrible thing happened. His father became very ill. Kamehameha trembled with fear as he stood outside his father's house. He could hear his father groaning while his many servants and warriors wailed and cried.

His mother called Kamehameha to her. Her face was pale and anxious. "There are wicked men here," she whispered. "Someone has poisoned your father, or put a spell on him. It's not safe for you anymore, my son. We don't know who our enemies are. I'm afraid that they are all around us. Hide in my house tonight, and stay out of sight."

Shivering, the boy crouched for long hours inside his mother's house, and then he heard the loud beat of drums. He peered out the door into the dark night. Warriors marched through the trees—many, many warriors, their brown bodies glistening with oil. A giant led them, a huge man standing over seven feet tall. "I am Puna," he said. "We have come from Ka'ū to fetch you, Kamehameha. Your uncle, Chief Kalani'ōpu'u, sent us."

That very night, surrounded by two hundred warriors, Nae'ole and Kamehameha were taken by war canoe to the fiery land of Ka'ū.

THE MYSTERIOUS LAND OF KA'Ū

The war canoe slid silently through black waves. Kamehameha stared into the darkness where a large mountain loomed. A strange burning smell made his nose itch, and in the distance fiery red lava burned a trail through the trees. "This is a strange land we are coming to, Nae'ole," he said.

The canoe settled on the black sand beach with a crunch. Other canoes followed. Suddenly rain poured down, and Nae'ole and Kamehameha scrambled for shelter. The huge party of warriors followed, huddling under the trees.

"Did you see the angry faces of Alapa'i and Keawe'opala?" a young warrior said, laughing. "I thought they would try to stop us from leaving."

"They didn't dare," a savage-looking warrior replied, thrusting his long spear hard into the ground. "We are men of Ka'ū and we are better than those cowards."

Puna grinned. "Ka'ū is the home of strong men, Kamehameha. It is the special place of the fire goddess, Pele." He pointed at the mountain. "That is where she lives."

A spray of fiery lava suddenly burst into the air. "Pele is angry tonight. Our people in Ka'ū love Pele, but we also fear her. Always remember that this is her land and pay her the proper respect. It's bad when she gets angry. Her hot lava can destroy all our crops and homes."

Puna led the way along a stone path that wound across the huge, black fields of spiky lava to a gulch where small grass houses crowded together under giant trees. Hundreds of kukui torches burned like little stars. Chief Kalani'ōpu'u came out of the largest house and embraced Kamehameha, welcoming him to Ka'ū. The chief's many wives stood behind him, smiling and murmuring.

"You're a big boy," Chief Kalani'ōpu'u said. "I hear they call you Kamehameha. That's a strong name. We'll train you to be a strong warrior. You'll be safe in Ka'ū. Go to sleep now. You must be tired."

Kamehameha crawled into the sleeping house. Too tired to think, he pulled the *kapa* cloth up until it covered his head and fell asleep.

The house was hot and still when he awoke. A warrior stood at the door. His shoulders were broad and his huge muscles bulged. Kamehameha recognized him and jumped up quickly; it was Kekūhaupi'o. Everyone knew of his battles. He could fight four spear-carrying men and still win.

"I've been sent to be your teacher," Kekūhaupi'o said. "Your uncle wants you to train to be a warrior. The training will be hard. Is this what you want?"

"Yes," Kamehameha said, nodding his head. "I want to learn to be a mighty warrior like you."

"We will do more than learn how to fight. To be a true leader you have to learn the history of our people—the long chants telling the names of your ancestors and all their great deeds. Also, you must learn the names of your enemies' ancestors and their deeds, so you will know how to conquer them."

"I will do it," Kamehameha said.

Kekūhaupi'o looked at him sternly. "You must learn about the stars, the seas, and the land."

"All right," Kamehameha agreed. He liked to watch the movements of the clouds and try to guess when it would rain. He wanted to know where birds flew and where fish gathered, and to learn to read the stars and navigate the oceans.

"You have to learn everything about the gods. As a royal leader you will care for the resources of the gods on earth."

Kamehameha nodded seriously. He wanted to learn everything about his favorite god, the war god Kū. He knew this powerful god could help him in battles.

"Don't worry," Kekūhaupi'o said. "There will be plenty of time for sport. Sport builds a strong body. Go now. Your cousins are waiting."

"Come, Kamehameha, come quickly!" Kepo'o called. "Pele has caused the earth and the ocean to rock, and the waves are great."

Kamehameha rushed to the door of the house. The air was yellow and smelled of smoke and sulfur. A low, rumbling noise came from the earth, and the ground moved under his feet. He grabbed hold of a tree to keep his balance. Pele was very angry!

The boys ran downhill to the sea, whooping with excitement. Huge, foaming waves crashed on the black sand beach. Kamehameha grabbed his heavy wooden surfboard and followed.

"Look!" Kepo'o shouted as they ran to the shore. "Pele's fire!" He pointed to the flood of liquid red fire pouring over the far cliffs into the ocean. Clouds of steam rose into the sky and the sea boiled and hissed as hot lava slid into it. More than twenty surfers rode the huge waves, naked and cheering. Kamehameha plunged into the warm, heaving water. This is the best surf ride of my life, he thought. Truly, Pele is a powerful goddess.

KAMEHAMEHA'S FIRST BATTLE

Bodies oiled and spears ready, the warriors paddled war canoes fast over the dark seas. Kamehameha was proud to be with the fighting men, glad that his Uncle Kalani'ōpu'u had said he could watch this battle. They were going to war against his childhood enemy, Keawe'opala. He remembered him well. King Alapa'i was dead, and Keawe'opala was now king of the Kona district. He was a weak king who made the people angry.

A red sun appeared over the sea as the warriors scrambled out of the canoes. Keawe'opala's warriors were waiting, lining the banks of the gulch.

"Come out and fight, you shrimp-head cowards," Kalani'ōpu'u shouted.

Kamehameha snorted with laughter.

Kalani'ōpu'u looked very grand with his red feather cloak and yellow feather helmet. He carried an image of Kū, the war god. Kū's dogteeth were glistening and his pearl shell eyes shone. “We will make pig’s food out of you,” Kalani‘ōpu‘u shouted, “and even the pigs will not eat you. We can smell you from here.”

Keawe‘opala’s warriors jeered back, lunging and making threatening gestures to show how strong they were. For a moment it all seemed to Kamehameha like an exciting game. Then the fighting started. “Stay back, Kamehameha,” Kalani‘ōpu‘u called. “I don’t want you in the fighting. Stay at the rear, and watch and learn.”

Kamehameha watched the fighting warriors and admired the bravery of Kekūhaupi‘o. He dodges the falling spears as if they were raindrops, he thought. They won the battle, and Kamehameha was eager to join the fighting men. His chance came soon, when Kalani‘ōpu‘u started a military campaign against Kahekili, the mighty tattooed chief of the island of Maui.

At last, Kamehameha was one of the fighting warriors! He was going to kill or be killed. His heart pounded with excitement as blood-curdling war shouts filled his ears. Kekūhaupiʻo pulled him onto a rock outcrop, his eyes narrowed as he calculated the best action. "We'll take the rear guard for the moment," he said.

A shield of fighting men battled in front of them. Kamehameha fired his sling stones furiously, aiming at the enemy chiefs whenever possible. Two long spears whistled by his head, and he dodged them. Hailstorms of stones from the slings of the Maui warriors came flying, and he ducked quickly. The enemy had gained ground.

On the frontlines, warriors fought with short spears and shark-tooth clubs; some panted and grunted in hand-to-hand combat. Clouds of red dust swirled over the battleground. With screams and roars filling his ears, Kamehameha aimed and flung his long spear at a club-whirling enemy. Suddenly, he saw Kekūhaupiʻo crash to the ground. Breathing a prayer to the great war god Kū, he ran to him. Kekūhaupiʻo was frantically twisting and pulling his foot, and Kamehameha saw it was caught in a sweet potato vine. An enemy warrior charged, dagger aimed and ready.

"Help! Kekūhaupiʻo is down!" Kamehameha yelled to the warriors nearest him. Warriors ran to protect Kekūhaupiʻo, clubs swinging and daggers thrusting.

Kekūhaupiʻo freed his foot, then swung his club in a vicious circle, driving off an approaching enemy. "Thank you, Kamehameha," he said, grinning, and charged back into the battle.

Kalaniʻōpuʻu's warriors won the battle, but Kamehameha knew it wouldn't be long before other war-loving chiefs attacked again. He knew there would never be peace until the islands were united under one leader. Long ago a powerful prophet had said that the man who moved the Naha Stone would be the greatest king of Hawaiʻi, and all the islands would be united under his control. Was this his destiny?

THE NAHA STONE

"You cannot move the Naha Stone, Kamehameha," Nae'ole said. "It weighs over five thousand pounds. It would be like trying to move a mountain. You are strong, but even a giant couldn't move that stone. He would need the magic of the gods."

"I have to move the stone," Kamehameha said.

"There is a powerful, sacred law protecting the stone. If you try to move it and fail, you will have offended the gods and the *kāhuna*, the priests, will put you to death."

"I won't fail," Kamehameha replied.

The Makahiki festival would be held in six months, and that would be the best time to try to move the stone. The Makahiki, held at the temple near the Naha Stone, was a time of feasting and games when people prayed to Lono, god of peace and farming. Lono's priests were not as fierce as the priests of the war god Kū. Kamehameha knew that the gods would decide if he was to succeed.

Kamehameha trained every day. He wrestled, threw the javelin and lifted his heavy old surfboard, which weighed as much as a big pig. He crawled underneath the twenty-man war canoe and pressed his back to it, trying to budge it. He arched his back and bent his knees to lift it. He could feel his muscles growing.

"You're crazy, Kamehameha," Kepo'o said. "If the *kāhuna* are angry, they will kill you. Even the *kāhuna* of Lono can get mad."

Rain poured down on the first day of the festival. More than four hundred people gathered in houses and on the open field. Some came from the mountain villages; others arrived by canoe. People laughed, talked, sang and ate as they walked around or stood under trees to escape the rain. A group of young men crowded around some massive wrestlers, cheering and yelling. The wrestlers showed their most fearsome faces and stuck out their tongues. Some of the people whispered when they saw Kamehameha. Somehow the news had spread that he was going to try to lift the stone.

"Here comes Kamehameha," a pretty girl said. "Let's see how he does."

"He comes to test if he will live a long life or die in the mud," a big man laughed.

Nae'ole had a worried look in his eyes as he and Kamehameha walked closer to the sacred stone. It was black and pitted and huge—bigger than a ten-foot surfboard and heavier than a twenty-man war canoe. *Kāhuna* sat in the nearby temple, guarding it. One of them watched Kamehameha, his eyes narrowed.

"I will come at night and try to move it," Kamehameha said quietly to Nae'ole. "That way, if I fail, no one will know."

That night, after midnight, Nae'ole and Kamehameha quietly circled the houses, hiding in the shadows of the bushes. Kukui torches flickered, lighting the darkness as they approached the stone. A tall, thin priest stood at its side, watching them warily.

Kamehameha gripped Nae'ole's arm. "Tomorrow," he said. "I'll move it tomorrow."

In the morning, the same *kahuna* guarded the stone. Again, he watched Kamehameha closely. Heart pounding, Kamehameha walked up to the stone, murmuring a prayer to Lono. Hearing the prayer to his god, the *kahuna* began to smile. Now was the time! Kamehameha grabbed the smaller end of the stone. He was shocked at how big it was close up. This was not going to be easy. Now he was committed—this would be a day of death or fame.

He gripped his legs around the stone and pushed with all his might. Nothing happened. The stone didn't budge. He was going to fail. Sweat poured down his face. He gave another mighty heave. Again, nothing happened.

Other priests ran forward, calling excitedly to each other. Streams of people followed them, curious about the reason for the commotion.

Kamehameha was breaking the *kapu* of the sacred Naha Stone. He was not of Naha descent and it was *kapu,* forbidden, for him to touch it. Nae'ole hurried forward, stumbling as he ran.

"Let's get out of here, Kamehameha," he shouted. "Come on! Let's go!"

Kamehameha panted, trying to catch his breath. Then, from the corner of his eye, he saw a wild-eyed *kahuna* come out of the temple, carrying the war god Kū. Kū's red feathers bristled in the wind and his fierce eyes gleamed. Did the *kahuna* think he was afraid of Kū? Kū was the war god he worshipped.

He braced his legs in the bowlegged stance of Kū and strained under the stone again. The huge boulder moved! He pushed it five feet from where it had been lying. The *kāhuna* muttered, whispering of magic powers. Kamehameha pressed his way underneath the slope of the stone and strained himself erect, until the stone stood almost upright. Then, with a mighty heave, he pushed it over!

The *kāhuna* and the spectators stared. Nae'ole clasped his hands together, gaping open-mouthed. Dust filled the air where the huge stone had crashed. Then people began to bow down, venerating Kamehameha as though he were already a king. He had won! The prophecy was true—he would be the mighty king of all the islands.

Kamehameha achieved his ambition. He grew into a gifted warrior chief who united the warring island chiefdoms into the peaceful and prosperous Hawaiian kingdom.

The young boy grew into a giant of a man, almost seven feet in height. He was a strong natural athlete; a powerful and fearless warrior; and a strong-minded, brilliant administrator. Ruthless in war and kind and forgiving when the need for fighting was past, Kamehameha made laws to protect both chiefs and commoners. He encouraged the people to farm and fish. He traded with foreign nations and was friendly to all nationalities, but always remained faithful to the Hawaiian culture and religion.

Statues of King Kamehameha stand in Kapa'au on the Big Island and in front of Ali'iōlani Hale in Honolulu. Kamehameha holds his spear in his left hand as a reminder that he brought hundreds of years of war to an end. His right hand is extended with his palm open in a gesture of the aloha spirit. A similar statue stands in the National Statuary Hall in Washington, D.C. A textbook used by the U.S. Military Academy at West Point ranks Kamehameha with Napoleon Bonaparte and Alexander the Great as a great military strategist.

The massive Naha Stone stands in front of the Hawai'i County Library in Hilo, Hawai'i.

BIBLIOGRAPHY

Desha, Stephen L. *Kamehameha and His Warrior Kekūhaupi'o.* Kamehameha Schools Press, Honolulu, Hawai'i, 2000.

Kamakau, S. M., *Ruling Chiefs of Hawai'i.* Kamehameha Schools Press, Honolulu, Hawai'i, 1964.

Mellen, Kathleen Dickenson, *The Lonely Warrior.* Hastings House, New York, New York, 1949.

Tregaskis, Richard, *The Warrior King.* Falmouth Press, Honolulu, Hawai'i, 1973.

Williams, Julie Stewart, *Kamehameha the Great.* Kamehameha Schools /Bernice Pauahi Bishop Estate, Honolulu, Hawai'i, 1993.